Benjamin Coates

Cotton cultivation in Africa: Suggestions on the Importance of the Cultivation of Cotton in Africa

SALZWASSER
VERLAG

Benjamin Coates

Cotton cultivation in Africa: Suggestions on the Importance of the Cultivation of Cotton in Africa

Reprint of the original, first published in 1858.

1st Edition 2023 | ISBN: 978-3-37514-814-0

Verlag (Publisher): Salzwasser Verlag GmbH, Zeilweg 44, 60439 Frankfurt, Deutschland
Vertretungsberechtigt (Authorized to represent): E. Roepke, Zeilweg 44, 60439 Frankfurt, Deutschland
Druck (Print): Books on Demand GmbH, In de Tarpen 42, 22848 Norderstedt, Deutschland

Cotton Cultibation in Africa.

SUGGESTIONS

ON THE IMPORTANCE OF THE

CULTIVATION OF COTTON IN AFRICA,

IN REFERENCE TO THE

ABOLITION OF SLAVERY IN THE UNITED STATES,

THROUGH THE ORGANIZATION OF AN

African Cibilization Society.

BY

BENJAMIN COATES.

PHILADELPHIA:
PRINTED BY C. SHERMAN & SON.
1858.

PREFACE.

THE suggestions on the importance of the cultivation of cotton in Africa, as a measure calculated to effect the abolition of slavery in America, were presented originally to those more immediately interested in the success of the proposed measure. The practicability of the scheme was then supposed to have been clearly demonstrated. But that which a few years since might have been considered rather speculative, and, perhaps, by some even visionary, with the information then obtained, is now placed beyond all doubt; and the fact is established to the entire satisfaction of those who have labored so zealously for the accomplishment of the object —that cotton of superior quality, fully equal to the best grown in America, can be raised in Africa by free labor, in an unlimited quantity, and much cheaper than it can be produced by the expensive slave labor of the United States. In confirmation of this, we have the testimony of the celebrated African travellers, Barth, Livingstone, and Bowen, whose explorations have revealed the fact that nearly the whole continent of Africa is admirably adapted to the cultivation of cotton. That in many places it grows spontaneously, and that several kinds bloom all through the year, requiring only the labor of picking. They establish another fact scarcely less important, both to Africa and to the world, viz., that most of the interior tribes are a very *industrious people*, not only willing, but glad to work for the smallest compensation. And that many of these natives are very intelligent, far superior in capacity, in morals, and industry to those on the coast, who have become demoralized in all respects by their intercourse with slave-traders.

In corroboration of this testimony, Thomas Clegg, of Manchester, England, a practical cotton spinner and large manufacturer, to whose indefatigable exertions the whole civilized world is much indebted for valuable information and experiments of the greatest importance to the cause of philanthropy and civilization, and the "Cotton Supply Association of Manchester," of which it is believed Mr. Clegg is a leading and active member, both give assurance of the value of this most important staple, and the cheapness at which it may be produced. Thus proving, beyond any doubt, that Africa possesses within herself all the means, not only for her own elevation and regeneration, but also for severing the bonds of slavery, to which her children are subjected in foreign lands.

It cannot be that any number of intelligent black men can be found who will shut out the claims of Africa to their sympathies; but with increased knowledge of the capabilities of the African continent, the great advantages it presents in many respects to enterprising colored emigrants from the United States, who can take with them the means for developing the resources of the country, and thus introduce in every successive year an improved civilization, must the interest in Africa increase.

The writer presents these remarks solely on his own responsibility; feeling a strong interest in the civilization and christianization of Africa, as well as in the welfare of the whole African race in the United States.

CULTIVATION OF COTTON IN AFRICA.

By the true philanthropist of the present day, whose sympathies are enlisted for the oppressed of all countries and of every race, any suggestion that may lead to even a partial improvement of their condition will be received with favor. And on the people of the United States chiefly rests the responsibility of discovering the best mode of emancipating four millions of bondmen in their midst; and of providing for their future welfare, when emancipated. This has been deemed so difficult a subject—so complex in its political, social, and economical bearings, that many well-disposed persons have been willing to pass it by, as a question to be solved by time, or by the superior wisdom of a future age; although aware that every successive year increases and strengthens the evil.

But there are some who believe that *the present* is the proper time for action, and that *they* have a duty to perform in this great work, that should not be neglected. To such it is desired to make a few suggestions, under a belief that, with proper effort, much may be done now to effect the desired result, and that measures may be commenced immediately, which will eventuate, at no distant period, in a general emancipation, without violence of any kind, and without any collision with the laws of the land.

As slavery originated in the spirit of gain, by which alone it is still sustained, it is proposed to make use of the same agency to accomplish its overthrow. It is generally conceded that the profit derived from the culture of Cotton is the chief support of slavery in America, and this being the most vulnerable point, is that towards which the attack on the institution should be directed; for whatever shall prove available in making slave labor unprofitable, must of course cause the demand for that labor to cease. It is proposed to accomplish this result by means of the cultivation of cotton in Africa, with the use of free labor. As the soil of Africa is much more fertile than that of the United States, and is particularly adapted to the growth of cotton, the advantages in its favor must be apparent to the most superficial observer; for not only can all the best varieties at present cultivated in the United States, be more cheaply raised in Western or Central Africa, but there are several kinds indigenous to that continent, of superior quality, that have been highly approved in the English market. When it is remembered that this plant is perennial in Africa, and produces very much more than it does in America, where it must be planted annually, the superiority of the former over the latter will be very obvious; but in comparing the cost of labor in the two countries, the difference is still greater in favor of the free labor of Africa, over the slave labor of America.

To make this apparent to the most skeptical, it is only necessary to compare the value of slaves in Africa, with the market price of the same class of laborers in the United States. The foreign slave-traders usually pay from twenty to fifty dollars for each slave, in trade-goods, at an enormous profit; so that the *cash* value of a good field-hand may be safely estimated at from fifteen to twenty-five dollars; while the same laborer in America would cost from five hundred to one thousand dollars. This comparison shows the real difference in the value of labor to be estimated in calculating the relative cost of the production of this important staple, the variation in the price of which so seriously affects our commercial prosperity as to make the information respecting it, of the first importance on every arrival from Europe. As this comparison, however, is only between slave labor in the two countries, and as the object of encouraging the increased production of cotton in Africa is to liberate the bondman there as well as here, some may be inclined to doubt whether the native African, in a state of freedom, can be so stimulated by the love of gain, and the hope of improving his condition, as to compete successfully with the compulsory labor used here. But it must be remembered how vast is the population of Africa, and that the employment of even a very small part of it, for a few hours each day, would give a greater amount of labor than that obtained by compulsion from the smaller number in the United States. And when we take into view, the difference in the cost of living, the exceeding productiveness of the soil, and that much less clothing is required in that tropical climate than with us, may we not reasonably calculate from these facts, that cotton, more than equal to the whole product of the United States, can be obtained from the free sons of Africa in their native land, at less than one-half of its present cost, while amply compensating the laborer, and, at the same time, greatly improving his condition in other respects? This plan is, then, simply to make the immense profits at present derived by the slave-trader from his iniquitous business, together with the great emolument accruing to the planter in the United States, from the unrequited labor of his slaves, both available to the African himself. And the same process that thus benefits the free laborer, as a necessary consequence, liberates the bondman in America, and emancipates the uncounted millions of slaves in Africa; for it is not to be supposed that slavery will continue long anywhere, when it is found to be unprofitable.

All the Bible arguments of southern theologians, or the patriotic appeals of pro-slavery politicians, will not avail to sustain an institution that occasions a clear loss to every individual connected with it. Both slavery itself and its adjunct, the fugitive slave law, will then be numbered with the things that were; instead of laws for the protection of this species of property, we shall see, as John Randolph predicted, the master running away from the slave. Succeeding generations will read the history of the present time in constant wonder that such an institution as human slavery could have existed so long among a professedly Christian and enlightened people, glorying, in an eminent degree, in the republican principles of their government.

Assuming, then, that the free labor of Africa may be made available, if properly applied, to the abolition of slavery in both countries, the question will naturally arise, as to the best mode of accomplishing so desirable an object in the shortest time possible; and also that the greatest amount of good, as well as the chief profit, shall result to the advantage of the entire African race.

To this end, care should be taken that the business of collecting, cleaning, pressing, and exporting the cotton, should not be monopolized either by English or American capitalists, nor by any associations of white men, with even very philanthropic views in regard to the abolition of slavery. The most suitable agents to promote the success of the measure, whose exertions could be made to advance their own interest and that of their posterity, while they were using the most effective measures for eradicating one of the greatest evils of the present age, are enterprising colored men from the United States, properly educated, so as to be qualified for the work, and who are capable of appreciating the immense benefits to the world that must result from their labors. These men could form settlements on the whole western coast of Africa, between the parallels of 20 deg. north and 20 deg. south latitude, which would include Upper and Lower Guinea and Gambia—selecting, of course, the most eligible points on the coast, not already possessed by other powers, from whence they could gradually extend themselves into the interior. They would thus be enabled to control the vast and continually increasing commerce of a hitherto unexplored region, comprising the larger and better portion of Central Africa—sufficient of itself, with the improvements in cultivation naturally introduced by civilization, to form a large and very lucrative portion of the commerce of the world.

The important results that must follow from the success of this scheme, cannot fail to strike every one who will give it attention. The downfall of American slavery is inevitable, and with it the whole system of servitude throughout the world; for, with the great advantage thus shown that Africa possesses for the cultivation of cotton, over the more expensive lands and labor in America, is it to be doubted for a moment that it can be *profitably raised at much less than one half of the price it has commanded in the United States for many years past?*

Cotton, however, is not the only article of general consumption produced by slave labor, that can be more cheaply cultivated in Africa by freemen. Coffee and rice grow there luxuriantly, and have already been raised to a considerable extent and with comparatively little labor; both being indigenous to that continent. The Liberia coffee is considered one of the best varieties in the English market, where it commands a high price, and for that reason but little is imported into the United States.

This plan for eradicating one of the greatest evils that afflicts so large a portion of the human race, and our

own country in particular, may seem so plain, when
viewed in the light of its commercial importance alone,
and yet so simple in the means proposed for carrying it
into effect, that many will be inclined to ask why it has
not been tried before, if so efficacious as here repre-
sented, for the accomplishment of its object? This
would be a natural question, and the answer is this:
The agents who would be best adapted to the work, in
most respects, have not been properly educated for it;
the influences surrounding them in this country have
all been of a depressing nature, calculated to discourage
any noble aspirations that would lead them to promote
the welfare of their race, and to achieve for it a higher
position in the estimation of the world than it has yet
attained; and from this want of a knowledge of their
own capabilities, they have been too long contented
with the most servile occupations.

The great mortality that occurred in some of the
earlier expeditions that formed the settlement of the
present republic of Liberia, has given rise to very in-
correct views as to the salubrity of the climate, and has
led the colored man to overlook the great advantages
that must result to himself, to his posterity, and to the
entire race, from a vigorous and judicious prosecution of
the scheme in the manner here indicated. It is, however, not desirable that a very large proportion of our
colored population should at once emigrate to Africa,
much less a general exodus; but if only fifty thousand
of the intelligent and educated should be induced to
settle there within the next ten years, what might they
not accomplish? This would be but *one-tenth* of the
free colored population of the United States, and only
equal to about one per cent. per annum. Yet this
number, distributed in some eight or ten different settlements along the coast, would form the nucleus of
probably as many independent States, hereafter to form
a confederacy similar to our own; and, as they would

naturally adopt republican principles, might in less than half a century show a more important destiny for this race, in the civilization and christianization of Africa, and perform a more important part in the great work of the world's redemption, than many of their best friends have ever anticipated. If it should be objected that this calculation is *not entirely within the bounds of moderation*, that the effects hoped for are too great for the means employed, we have only to look at our own country to see the vast results of colonization from small beginnings; or to realize what has been accomplished within the last few years in California and Australia; and then ask ourselves if the colored man has not greater inducements, at this time, to emigrate to Africa, than our forefathers had, in their day, to emigrate to America? And is the prospect of gain that yearly takes so many thousands to the gold fields of California and Australia, to be compared with the great advantages accruing to the enterprising emigrant to Western Africa?

If any one doubts the capability of colored men to overcome difficulties in establishing for themselves an independent government, and in spreading the blessings of civilization and christianity among savage people, he has only to cast his eyes on Liberia to see what has been achieved by a few thousand of the same class, a large majority of whom were emancipated slaves, without any previous education or the least experience in the great work they have so successfully accomplished. Liberia has fully established the capacity of the African race for self-government and the highest degree of civilization, and she stands at this moment as the most successful example of colonization to be found in the annals of history.

There we see an independent government, formed on strictly republican principles, modelled after our own in all respects, *slavery excepted*, established and creditably conducted by less than ten thousand of the African race, most of them from a state of bondage in America, and of whom not one hundred ever had an education in this country such as is to be obtained in our best schools. They were aided, indeed, in the first instance, by the labors of a few of the self-denying and devoted friends of this oppressed people, among whom the names of Ashmun and Buchanan should be held in grateful remembrance by every true-hearted black man in Africa or America.

Liberia is now enjoying a high degree of prosperity, and occupies an honored and most respectable position among the civilized governments of the world, her sovereignty and independence having been acknowledged by Great Britain, France, Prussia, Belgium, Brazil, Hamburg, Lubec, Bremen, and Portugal, with all of whom she interchanges national civilities, and a mutually lucrative trade; her flag and her revenue laws are respected by the vessels of all nations, and her citizens meet on equal terms those from Europe or America who visit her ports in pursuit of commerce, or in the employment of their respective countries. On the two occasions when her chief magistrate visited Europe, he was received with distinguished consideration by the nobility and crowned heads, and by the virtuous of other classes of the most powerful and most refined nations of the Eastern Continent. Liberia, however, still needs the sympathy and aid of her friends in extending the benefits of education among her growing population, as both the government and people are far from a state of affluence. Yet, they have overcome most of the difficulties incident to the settlement of a new country, especially that great obstacle, the slave-trade, with which they had to contend for many years, and which resisted them with all its power, constantly inciting the natives to oppose their friendly and peaceful advances. The slave-trade is now entirely destroyed, not only within their own borders, but it is prohibited in *all* their treaties with the native kings who have sought their friendship. The Liberians have otherwise exerted a healthful influence in the suppression of wars between the different tribes with whom they have had intercourse.

When it is remembered that the entire yearly consumption of cotton in England alone is upwards of 800,000,000 of lbs., and of this 79 per cent., or more than three-fourths, is raised in the United States, it will be readily perceived how indispensable it is that we should undermine this powerful support of slavery, in our plans for the overthrow of the institution. This done, we may safely leave the repeal of all fugitive slave laws, and the answer to all pro-slavery arguments, to the slaveholders themselves. Make slavery obviously unprofitable, and the work is done.

In this view of the case, our first and great duty would seem to be, to raise the colored man from his present state, infuse into him a noble ambition to occupy a more elevated position in the world, and to qualify him to act the part which appears to be so clearly marked out for him in this age of progress.

With a liberal education, it is not to be supposed that he will fail to recognize the responsibility resting on him, and learn to know that it is on his own exertions he must mainly depend to become a useful and respected member of society; he will then see the importance of immediate action, to secure for himself and his children some of the advantages that the Continent of Africa offers to the enterprising emigrants who seek her shores; and having thus secured a home for themselves, and laid the foundation of an extensive Christian empire, will soon be able to receive all of their brethren whose interest or adventurous spirit may lead them to seek a new abode from under the dominion of "the proud and imperious Saxon," where their labor will be estimated at its proper value. Our duty, however, will be but

partially performed to a long-neglected portion of our
brethren, by freeing them from actual bondage, without,
at the same time, making provision for their future welfare. We must bear in mind that the prejudice arising
from a long course of degradation will not soon be
eradicated after chattel slavery shall have ceased; that
while we may grant them entire equality under the law,
in accordance with our republican creed, yet that social
equality which cannot be looked for until the feeling of
brotherly love, engendered by a truer spirit of Christianity than at present prevails, shall have pervaded the
mass of the community; and as this work will be a
work of years, many of the free spirits among our
colored brethren may not be willing to await this "good
time coming." When the certainty of a general emancipation is made manifest to our Southren brethren,
it is to be hoped that there will be shown a liberal
and Christian spirit toward their slaves, that will induce them to allow such educational privileges as will
prepare them to become useful, either in the land of
their nativity or that of their adoption. Many, no doubt,
will still be employed as laborers in the Southern States,
where their services, to a certain extent, will be indispensable, while others will seek new residences, in which
they can immediately become landed proprietors. To
provide for a large emigration of this nature, consequent
upon the success of the measures indicated for the overthrow of slavery, a broad and sure foundation should be
laid, upon which these new African States will be
erected.

In asking the attention of the friends of the African
race to this subject, it is respectfully suggested, that
much may be done towards the object at the present
time, by extending the facilities of education to the
different towns and settlements in Liberia, in establishing primary, high, and normal schools for both males
and females, and also by furnishing each settlement

with the necessary machines for cleaning and pressing cotton. These must be extended as new settlements are formed, as the emigrants are generally very poor, and require all their means for the cultivation of their farms. Capital is, therefore, much needed by them for such purposes. To secure the accomplishment of this plan on a scale commensurate with the important end to be attained, combined effort will be necessary; and as the measures proposed do not come within the prescribed duties of any existing organization, the object will probably be effected in the surest manner by a union of all the friends of freedom in America, whose sympathy for the oppressed is not limited by geographical boundaries or national sovereignty, in an association with the philanthropists of Great Britain (or in such manner as shall receive their co-operation); and as distinguishing the society, and explaining its object, it might be called "The African Civilization Society." It would occupy a different field of labor from any other anti-slavery association, and thus be free from the objection of many, whose exertions have been limited to mere partial measures. There are in the religious Society of Friends, many who deeply feel the wrongs of slavery, and who would gladly avail themselves of an opportunity of more extended usefulness, but who have not deemed it their duty to take an active part in the political conflict that the slavery question has engendered. Such will probably see in this quiet and peaceful, yet most effective mode of overcoming the principal obstacle to our national prosperity, the way made clear for extending more enlightened views of governmental policy to the nations of the world, some of whom have been deterred from adopting our professed principles from the inconsistency of our practice, in continuing an institution at variance with both the obvious precepts of Christianity and our boasted republicanism.

The attention of the reader is called to the very rapid

development of the resources of Africa, particularly as shown in the vast increase in the exports of cotton within the past three years, through the agency of native Africans, stimulated thereto by the enterprise of British commerce, and British manufactures. It will also be noticed that the intelligent natives of Central Africa are not content with exporting only the raw material, but are already supplying foreign countries with it in its manufactured state, the product of their own skill and industry. If so much can be accomplished with so little effort by a semi-civilized people, and who have been viewed by some as incapable of taking care of themselves, and by others as so lacking both the industry and enterprise that actuates the white races, what may not reasonably be expected from this people under a superior state of civilization, and stimulated not only by the love of gain and the love of power, which is common to all men, but also by those nobler impulses which a pure Christianity is calculated to produce, when the higher objects of love to God and love to man shall supersede the inferior motives that actuate those of every race, who cannot appreciate the blessings of the highest civilization?

Here, then, is presented to the educated and Christian Afric-American, the instrumentality for abolishing slavery in America, and also of regenerating a whole continent, and placing a long-neglected race in a most favorable light before the nations of Christendom.

Will American Christians of African descent, secure the opportunity now offered, and in the most effective, yet peaceful way, strike a deathblow to slavery, to superstition, and crime, at the same time, by introducing Christianity into Central Africa, accompanied as it will be by the arts and science of civilized life? Several hundred missionaries, of various Christian denominations, from Europe and America, are now occupying this important field, and sowing the good seed; the harvest promises to be so bountiful, that more laborers are needed; and the natives, conscious of their inadequate means for so great a task, are now imploring some of their brethren in America to come over and help them. But it must be remembered that at present it is only the skilled laborers that are needed to gather the material as well as the spiritual harvest, for unskilled laborers, and rude materials they possess in abundance. American laborers, of higher culture, and American implements, of the most approved inventions, are required for the work; and when the harvest is gathered, then, no doubt, others will be invited to the feast.

So much has already been said and written on the subject of slavery, that what seems now most needed is argument addressed to the *pocket* as well as to the conscience of the slaveholder, and it is earnestly suggested that now is the time to *act*. Indeed, the time for talking on this subject seems to have passed, and action is now demanded. The action here contemplated is that of a perfectly legitimate commerce, stimulated not only by self-interest but also by Christian philanthropy, and is of such a character as to commend itself to the approbation of all right thinking men. It is only necessary that the colored population of the United States should fully appreciate their own power, so as to exercise it judiciously for the extinction of slavery and for the elevation of their race; but this can only be accomplished by organization, and to some extent, a united action: the motto of the United States should be their motto, "United we stand, divided we fall." To this end, therefore, the author would propose the formation of emigrant aid societies in each State, after the plan of the emigrant aid societies that settled Kansas (and which Hon. Eli Thayer is now so successfully prosecuting in Virginia), to form settlements in Yoruba, Soudan, and other portions of the high table land of Central Africa, which is described by recent explorers as both healthy and fertile, and free

2

from the vicinity of the mangrove swamps, which are the cause of the fever of the African coast.

It is very important that between these State associations there should be harmonious action, so as not to conflict with each other; this could be best insured by a general organization, to be styled "The African Civilization Society," to be composed either exclusively, or chiefly of men of known character and standing, who possess the confidence of the whole community. This should be entirely free from any party or sectarian bias, and thus be removed from the objections that might otherwise attach to it. Such a society should not be identified with any existing organization, while it would combine within itself the best features and missionary spirit of the colonization enterprise, with the philanthropic spirit of the various anti-slavery associations, so that of a natural consequence, if wisely conducted, it will supersede them all. An African Civilization Society then, formed on purely Christian principles, and conducted in accordance therewith, will enlist the sympathy and receive the aid and encouragement of all the true friends of the colored race, both in America and in Africa. Should such a society be located either in New York or Philadelphia as central points, there should still be auxiliaries in the different States, acting through the parent or principal organization. Such State societies could, from time to time, send out select companies of enterprising men who desire a change of residence for themselves and their children. These would be no filibustering expeditions to usurp power and dominion by force, but would go at the earnest solicitation of their semi-civilized brethren, taking with them the plough, the loom, and the anvil, with the arts and attainments of civilized life, as co-laborers with them in the great and glorious work of regenerating Africa.

A few picked men are all that will be required to produce this vast change; and the movement, therefore, should have no effect to unsettle or alarm the great mass of our colored population, whose rights should be respected here in the land of their birth, and their interest here promoted in every proper way.

But should only one person out of every hundred emigrate to Africa yearly, for the next ten years, it would be quite as many as could well be provided for; and, if they are of the right stamp, quite sufficient to work out great results to the world. While it is fully conceded that the great mass of the colored population of the United States will require that education, for years to come, which they can receive in this country better than in any other to which they might remove, notwithstanding all the difficulties and discouragements that surround them here, yet there are many who feel that their energies have not the opportunity they require in this land, and desire a broader field for the development of their talents. The question, then, is, whether such men shall be encouraged to grapple with difficulties that may be overcome by industry and perseverance, where their exertions will be amply rewarded. The success of these pioneers, in the great work of civilization, will give encouragement and strength to their brethren in America, who will thus acquire greater confidence in their own powers to work for the elevation of their race in America, as their friends are doing in Africa..

No one knows of how much he is capable, until there is something to call forth his energies. It is great occasions that make great men. What would Washington and Jefferson have been, except for the American Revolution? respectable Virginia gentlemen; and Adams, and Hancock, and their associates? honored citizens of Massachusetts. Who would have known of Roberts and Benson, further than as worthy colored men in America, but for the establishment of the republic of Liberia? And would not Frederick Douglass still be an unruly slave on a Maryland plantation, or working in a shipyard at New Bedford, except for the anti-slavery movement? And how many such men may there be, whose talents now lie dormant, who might largely benefit the world, should circumstances occur to cause their development, no one can say. But we would ask, is it anticipating too much to suppose that a yearly emigration of only one out of a hundred of our free colored population, which would be about five thousand persons, from among the most enterprising and energetic among them, even if not all of superior education, yet going as farmers, merchants, and mechanics, of the various trades, with their churches and schools, and forming settlements among the intelligent natives of Yoruba, of Soudan, of Dahomey, and Ashantee, should be the means of Christianizing that whole district of country, and effect, in a few years, a peaceful revolution, such as the world has never seen.

This emigration movement is essentially different from any that has ever before taken place. Here are people of the same race going to those who will receive them with open arms, and who are most desirous to be benefited by the religion, the commerce, and the improved civilization of their more advanced brethren. An emigration of one per cent. per annum of our free colored population to Africa, will place fifty thousand civilized men there in the next ten years; and surely one man out of one hundred would scarcely be missed in America. Yet what could they not accomplish for Africa? Who does not believe that even one thousand civilized men from America, forming settlements in either Dahomey or Ashantee, would be sufficient to place Christianity in the ascendant, and cause a peaceful revolution in either or both of those kingdoms in much less than ten years? Why, then, should we not have a confederacy of republican states in Africa, that shall control the immense commerce of the interior of that continent, and supply cotton sufficient for the wants of the world?

The vast importance of the commerce of Africa is such to the manufacturing nations of·Europe, who also need her cotton, coffee, and sugar, that the spirit of avarice that has led the white man to America, and to Australia, and the grasping power of England, which has seized India and China, will also take possession of Central Africa, now that its great wealth and healthy climate have become known, unless it is at once settled by the colored men of America. The question, then, simply is, shall Africa be possessed and controlled by the white man or the black man? Shall the former always maintain the superior, and the latter an inferior position? or will the black man assert his equal right, at least in Africa? And when having firmly secured to its original possessors the benefit of their own toil and labors, and shall have employed that wealth and power, thus acquired, to the civilization of the entire continent, and the spread of true Christianity, not only to all within its borders, but to those of every color and every race, they will thus not only break the fetters of the slave, but will be the means, under Divine Providence, of advancing and securing the rights of all men.

If the greatness of this work, with the full assurance of the importance of the results that must ensue from their rightly directed labors, shall fail to inspire the colored men of America with a determination to succeed in their glorious mission, it is difficult to conceive of higher and nobler objects that can arouse their dormant energies, and impel them to a brighter future.

TESTIMONY.

MR. CLEGG'S LETTER.

THE following letter on the success which has attended Mr. Clegg's persevering efforts to promote the cultivation of cotton on the West Coast of Africa was recently addressed by that gentleman to Mr. McGregor Laird, the promoter of the new commercial expedition up the Niger. The facts are highly encouraging.

MANCHESTER, March 18, 1858.

MY DEAR SIR:

I may state that my operations in Africa were commenced, some seven or eight years ago, with the view of putting down the slave-trade by a new but very simple method, viz., convincing the native African chiefs and others that it was their interest to employ their people, instead of making war upon each other for the sake of getting a colorable right or pretext for selling into slavery the prisoners taken in such marauding expeditions. I commenced at Sierra Leone, and strongly recommended every one to begin to collect the cotton already growing, and to cultivate more wherever it would grow. The Church Missionary Society kindly recommended agents to conduct the business, and in every way aided my efforts with the very great influence they so deservedly possess. The African Native Agency Committee of London kindly paid the agents their salaries, and the African Improvement Society of Sierra Leone put down an hydraulic packing-press, made by Messrs. Bellhouse, of Manchester, to pack such cotton as these agents and others might be able to purchase. Not being able to collect more than about two hundred and thirty-five pounds of clean cotton during the first year, I found that Sierra Leone was not the right place at which to try the experiment, and at once decided to go direct to the interior cotton-field, and to the residence of the chiefs about Abbeokuta. In the meantime I discovered that all our European agents either died off or had to return to this country, and another long process had to be gone through, by which several more years were almost lost. The Missionary Society kindly selected several young Africans, who came over to this country at the expense of the Native Agency Committee, to be educated and instructed in the best method of cleaning the cotton without injury to the fibre. Two of these I had at my mill in the country for several years, where they also learned to work as mechanics, carpenters, &c.; a third I had in my office in town as clerk, bookkeeper, &c. In the meantime another young African, who had been educated as a surgeon in England, took the matter up heartily, and conducted the various transactions until the two others from the mill returned to their own country. These three native African youths have since conducted the whole of my operations in a manner most creditable to themselves and their country. The African Native Agency Committee of London liberally supplied several packing-presses, a boat, weighing-machines, cotton stores, and other heavy articles, whilst I supplied cotton-gins, goods, and money to purchase the cotton with. Consul Campbell, of Lagos, seeing the great advantage likely to accrue to Africa from the energetic prosecution of the new trade, rendered every assistance; indeed, he applied for, and has obtained leave from Government to come over to this country, and may be expected this spring to come down to Manchester—where I hope he will be my guest—with a view to further and promote these operations under the sanction of our Government.

Up to the first of the month, I have sent out one hundred and fifty-seven cotton-gins, costing from 3*l*. 17*s*. 6*d*. to 10*l*. 10*s*. each. I have entered into correspondence with upwards of seventy-six native and other African traders—twenty-one or twenty-two of them being chiefs —many of whom have begun to consign their cotton, as well as other produce, to me; and I assure you it gives me the greatest pleasure to sell it for the highest price I can obtain, as well as to invest the money in any articles they may require, with the exception of spirits, or the implements of war. In conducting this affair, I have to venture, and have now outstanding, about 4693*l*., every shilling of which I expect to receive back; indeed, I have bills of lading, and advices of great quantities of cotton and other produce being on its way to me now, both on consignment and in liquidation of what is owing to me. I have had one transaction with one of these traders from which he received 3500*l*.; and it is both satisfactory and pleasing to know that every trader almost invariably takes back hardware, earthenware, cotton goods, or other merchandise, for the whole amount of cotton or other produce sent here. Owing to two extensive fires at Abbeokuta, I have not got quite as much cotton as I expected in 1857, but have had cotton advices and bills of lading for shipments from Lagos up to the 28th of December, as follows, viz.:

		Bales.
Per Candace,	. . . .	46
Gambia,	. . . .	19
Invincible,	. . . .	34
Token,	. . . .	36
Jarrow,	. . . .	41
Gambia,	. . . .	116
St. George,	. . . .	81
Powerful,	. . . .	249
Oscar,	. . . .	37
Saltern Rock,	. . . .	245
Propeller,	. . . .	34
In the whole,		929

	Bales.
Add to these 17 tons burnt in the first fire, and 3000 lbs. to 4000 lbs. in the second, ...	321
Produced, or rather collected for sending to me, of usual size, ... of African cotton.	1250

This quantity has therefore been purchased, and there has still always been *plenty more offering* on like terms, viz., $\frac{1}{2}d$. per lb. in the seed. On this account the people of Abbeokuta cannot be made to believe that England can purchase all the cotton that they can produce, and yet Abbeokuta is but just on the border, at one corner I may say, of the great cotton-field of Western Africa, extending from Abbeokuta to the Niger, and away into the interior. Coupling my experience on this coast, the belief of the Abbeokutans, and the recent despatch of Dr. Baikie from the Niger to our Government, where he states that the Rev. Mr. Clark had seen at Illa, near Ilorin, in the Yoruba country, fifteen or sixteen packages of clean cotton offered for sale, weighing seventy-five to eighty pounds each, and had been assured by the natives that on market-days (every fourth), from one to two thousand such bags were offered for sale, and this for their own country manufacture only: I say, coupling these statements with my operations, what I know of Tunis and Natal, and what Dr. Livingstone tells us of the East, I can clearly see a prospect of the slave-trade being entirely starved out; the tractable, docile, and intelligent African rising in the scale of civilization and Christianity in proportion as he is allowed to enjoy his own rights, stay in, till the land, and trade in his own native country, even if confined to the cultivation of cotton alone. You know, much better than I do, what Africa so abundantly produces beside cotton, such as palm and other oils, arrow-root, ground-nuts, ivory, cayenne pepper, fruits, spices, gums, resins, dyes, dye-woods, &c. I should give a poor idea of the prospect of the cotton-trade by simply mentioning the commencement and recent operations connected with my own experiment; for, in all such cases, people first look on, and when they clearly see advantage, they also set to work: so it has been, and so I wish it to be, in Western Africa. One trader has ordered a good, serviceable English canoe, to convey the cotton, whilst he and another have ordered each a good new packing-press, at considerable expense; and as there are now at least four presses ready for work, and the natives are able of themselves to turn out ten bales daily from each press, they should turn out forty daily, or upwards of 12,000 annually with their present appliances. Three makers of cotton-gins at Manchester, through my and various other instrumentality, have sent out to Africa the following, viz.:

Gins.						Lbs.
C. 34	capable of cleaning	100	daily, say for safety,	80		2720
D. 66	"	100	"	80		5280
J. 150	"	40	"	40		6000
250	capable of continuously cleaning daily					14,000

of clean cotton; 4363 lbs. yearly; 10,000 American, or 40,000 African-sized bales of cotton. And as all these gins have been bought, and in most instances paid for on delivery, I believe they will not be allowed to be idle. This, I think, is a rare instance of rapid development of a particular trade, and the more so, inasmuch, as in my case, every ounce of cotton has been collected, all the labor performed, and the responsibility of doing it borne by native Africans alone. I have many reasons for believing that the whole matter will prosper; first, I believe it has God's blessing upon it; next, Africa is naturally adapted for growing cotton, as everywhere it springs spontaneously, and is indigenous to the country; next, because wherever cotton will grow, the people cry out for the African to come and help them to cultivate it, showing, in my opinion, that he is its natural cultivator also. Besides all this, I find that African cotton—whether from Quilimane on the east, Abbeokuta on the west, Tunis or Algeria on the north, or Natal in the south—that this cotton is the best substitute for American cotton. Indeed, from whatever part of Africa it comes, in its natural state, it will invariably fetch in the Liverpool market from 2d. to 3d. per pound more than East-India cotton under similar circumstances. For some years this cotton has never cost more than ½d. per pound in the seed, and at that price the agents, chiefs, and dealers have never been able to buy up what has been offered; and this, I think, is a proof that it can be produced exceedingly cheap, sufficiently so to compete with any other country. It can be laid down in Liverpool in all ordinary times at about 4¼d. per pound, viz. :

	d.
Cost of it in the seed ½d. 4 lbs. to make one, . . .	2
Cleaning 30 to 40 lbs. for 4d., say, ...	¼
Packing and canvas, ...	½
Carriage and charges on board, ...	¼
Freight to England (too much by half), . . .	1
Charges in England, ...	¼
	4¼

Recently, however, the Native Agency Committee have begun to charge those who use their gins and pack in their store 1d. per pound, and those who do this will be at a little more expense; but as the cotton is still worth 7d. in Liverpool, and not long ago was worth 9d., there is yet profit sufficient to encourage all natives to embark in the trade. Believing first in the goodness of the cause, and next that to act entirely through the natives is the way not only further to develope, but most certainly the most sure way of making it progressive and lasting; also, having a dread that if Europeans took up the cultivation of cotton, or dealing in the interior, it would, in all probability, result in the revival of slave labor, or merely in a spasmodic effort or two, and then a sickening off, a failure, and relinquishing the effort, after destroying, in all probability, the self-reliance the native formerly had.

On these grounds, then, I am anxious to raise at least 2040*l.* for four new cotton stations, and I hand you an estimate for them which has been prepared by one who knows Africa, and what is requisite, much better than I do. It is as follows :

	£
20 gins, at 5*l.* each,	100
Press,	90
Weighing machine,	20
Shed, or native house,	100
Wages for two natives, one year,	100
Capital to trade with,	100
Or, for each station,	510

I feel that I have not half done justice to this matter, and only regret that I have not been well enough either to do it better now, or attend to it earlier. I must, therefore, supplement the statement by sending a few of my letters to the public papers, leaving you to deal with the whole in any manner most likely to redound to the benefit of Africa and this particular movement.

Yours, very truly,

(Signed)   THOMAS CLEGG.

McGREGOR LAIRD, ESQ.

ADDRESS BY MR. CAMPBELL.

THE subjoined extracts from a report from the London Times, of August 7th, 1858, of a meeting held on the preceding evening, in the Manchester Town Hall, on the subject of an increased supply of cotton from Africa, is deserving of mention, on account of the important facts stated by Mr. Campbell, British Consul at Lagos, and a resident for thirty-five years of Western Africa.

MR. CAMPBELL remarked:

" The palm-oil trade from the Bight of Benin had increased, during the last six years,* by about 600,000*l.* out of 1,000,000*l.* Why should not a cotton trade receive equal development if this country supplied capital for the purchase, and skill for the preparation of that important product? The first ship loaded with cotton would give the signal for the whole of the cotton regions of Africa. The people were exceedingly fond of agriculture. In Abbeokuta they preferred working in the plantations for 3*d.* a-day to working at any other employment for 9*d.* But hitherto they had been shut out from communication with civilized countries, and their roads were at present mere pathways. He believed the Niger would become the Mississippi of Africa as its trade became developed. At present the cotton from that region had been obtained from Abbeokuta only. It was a peculiar feature in this part of Africa, that it contained' towns of 40,000, 60,000, 80,000, 100,000, and even 120,000 inhabitants, while other parts only contained scattered villages. The people were not only growers, but manufacturers of cotton, and from Lagos and the Bight of Benin 200,000 cotton cloths of native manufacture, averaging 2½ lbs. each in weight, had been exported, in the year 1857, to the Brazils or elsewhere, for the clothing, probably, of their own countrymen. The shipment of cotton from Lagos, in 1856, was 34,491 lbs., and in 1857 it was 114,844 lbs. Small as these beginnings were, it was obvious how they were progressing. Besides the export, the people supplied their neighbors with at least 200,000 heavy cloths, weighing 4½ or 5 lbs. each. All this commerce had been established before we had begun to deal with them. He looked forward to our buying the cotton from the natives, and their purchasing from us the manufactured article, which we could supply so much cheaper. There was nothing to fear on the score of security to property. Europeans were everywhere received with kindness, and cotton was found exposed for sale in every town at the weekly markets. It might, therefore, be said that it was going a begging for want of purchasers. What was wanted by the growers and traders was the cheap and rapid means of cleaning the cotton. There was no foundation for the prevailing belief that the free African would not work if he were secured the fruits of his labor. At Lagos the people went to work at daybreak, and took their meals and rest in the heat of the day, and a more industrious people he believed did not exist. He had mentioned the value of labor at Abbeokuta, but at other towns it was only 2d. a day, or 1½d. a day in the interior. He estimated the population at a million and a half, and they were all clothed in garments of their own manufacture. He was confident that 4½ lbs. taken as the cotton consumption of each person was an extremely low estimate. In the question of cotton supply to England, it must be remembered that in Africa there was no rent to pay for the land. After referring to the importance of the indigo production of this part of Africa, and to the additional advantages it possessed, as regards cotton cultivation, that no lands have yet been cleared exclusively for that purpose, Mr. Campbell concluded by submitting detailed suggestions for the commencement of operations for promoting the cultivation of cotton in the districts in question, by sending a respectable man as superintending agent at Abbeokuta, with a supply of small presses, gins, an iron store, iron canoes to convey cotton bales between Abbeokuta and Lagos, &c. The agent should carry with him 2500l. or 3000l. in suitable merchandise for the purchase of cotton. He should be authorized to buy on the spot from time to time, as wanted, cowrie shells to the value of 250l., those being the currency of the country. They were to be had at Lagos from 22l. to 23l. the ton. The London and Liverpool market might be tried. The cheap blue shell cowries from Zanzibar were what was required, but care should be taken in selecting them, as, being bought by weight and sold by number, the smaller size shell would be the most profitable. The agent should be authorized to hire native sub-agents for the interior towns, men of good character; and as these did not abound, their services were now valued at from 60l. to 80l. per annum, they providing for themselves. The agent should be supplied with an iron house, lined inside with board, raised on iron pillars at least twelve feet high. This elevation was essential to health."

EXTRACT FROM BARTH'S TRAVELS.

"I MET with fertile lands, irrigated by large navigable rivers and extensive central lakes, ornamented with the finest timber, and producing various species of grain, rice, sesamum, ground-nuts in unlimited abundance, the sugar-cane, &c., together with COTTON and indigo, the most valuable commodities of trade. The whole of Central Africa, from Bagirme to the east as far as Timbuktu to the west (as will be seen in my narrative), abounds in these products. The natives of these regions not only weave their own cotton, but dye their home-made shirts with their own indigo."—*Preface*, pages 20, 21.

Barth describes his travels as " extending over a tract of country of twenty-four degrees from north to south, and twenty degrees from east to west, in the broadest part of the Continent of Africa."

DR. LIVINGSTONE'S TESTIMONY.

WHILE in England, Dr. Livingstone met the members
of the Chamber of Commerce, Commercial Association,
and Cotton Supply Association, at the Town Hall, Manchester, and in reply to questions put to him replied,
as thus reported by the London Times:

"In Angola, the natives knew of a very great many different dyes, which they were not very willing to make
known to Europeans. The Columba root was exported
by the Americans in abundance as a dye stuff, and grew
along the Zambesi River. Besides this, there was,
throughout the country, indigo, the kind called silver
indigo, with which the people dyed their clothes, and
which grew wild, for it was not at all cultivated. The
only exportation of it was by the Portuguese who lived
at Tete, but it might be exported abundantly.

In reference to cotton, Dr. Livingstone added, that
very large quantities of it were cultivated by the natives,
and one small district, between the Rivers Conza and
Loanda, produced 1300 cloths annually, of cotton grown
by the natives, spun by the women, and woven by the
men. The natives never employed any manure, and
the more the ground was worked the more fertile it became. The whole of Angola, if it had been in the hands
of Englishmen, for its size, would have produced much
more cotton and sugar than any part of the Southern
States of America. It grew abundantly on the west,
and that was by far the best field for cotton. On the
east it was cultivated a little, but it was not so good.
It clung to the seed, and an iron roller had to be used
to separate it. The quantity grown on the east side
was very much smaller than that on the west side, but
the natives had never been induced to cultivate cotton;
they had never been offered anything for it, and they

only cultivated a little to make clothes for themselves. He believed if they had a market they would cultivate largely, for wherever they had the opportunity of selling anything, they immediately began to collect it. In Angola skilled labor was to be had for 4d. a day, field labor for 2d., and he believed it might be got, by paying in calico, the usual currency of the country, at about 1d. a day. He proposed, on going back, to distribute cotton seeds among all the chiefs on the banks of the river, and endeavor to give the impression that all they produced would be purchased. The beginning must necessarily be small and not profitable, but he thought if the natives could be engaged in lawful commerce, it would put an end to the slave-trade in all that central region.

VIEWS OF ENGLISH STATESMEN.

The months of June and July last were fertile in Parliamentary discussions on the slave-trade and kindred subjects. Among these were repeated reference to the cultivation of cotton in Africa, a few of which are herewith presented. We quote from the London Times' report of proceedings.

S. FITZGERALD, Under Secretary of State, said:
He did not scruple to say that, looking at the papers which he had perused, it was not to India, it was not to other parts of the world which had been named, that we must direct our attention; it was to the West Coast of Africa that we must look for that large increase in our supply of cotton which was now becoming absolutely necessary, and without which he and others who had studied this subject foresaw grave consequences to the most important branch of the manufactures of this

3

country. In the papers which had been laid upon the table he found that our consul at Lagos reported:

" The whole of the Yoruba and other countries south of the Niger, with the Houssa and the Nuffe countries on the north side of that river, have been from all time cotton-growing countries; and, notwithstanding the civil wars, ravages, disorders, and disruptions caused by the slave-trade, more than sufficient cotton to clothe their populations has always been cultivated, and their fabrics have found markets and a ready sale in those countries where the cotton plant is not cultivated, and into which the fabrics of Manchester and Glasgow have not yet penetrated. The cultivation of cotton, therefore, in the above-named countries is not new to the inhabitants; all that is required is to offer them a market for the sale of as much as they can cultivate, and by preventing the export of slaves from the seaboard render some security to life, freedom, property, and labor."

He would not go into the items of the calculation, but it appeared from the statement made by this gentleman, that during the last year there were exported from this coast to the Brazils no less than 7,200,000 lbs. of cotton and cotton goods. He implored the House to consider what this trade might be made if, in the words of our consul, by repressing the slave-trade we gave security to labor and property. Another of our consuls, speaking of the trade in the Bight of Benin in 1856, said:

" The readiness with which the inhabitants of the large town of Abbeokuta have extended their cultivation of the cotton plant merits the favorable notice of the manufacturer, of the philanthropist, and, as a means of supplanting the slave-trade, by its turning the attention of the native to the value of the soil and of human labor, of her Majesty's Government."

It was worthy of notice that while the quantity of cotton obtained from America between 1784 and 1791, the first seven years of the importation into this country, was only 74 bales, during the years 1855 and 1856 the town of Abbeokuta alone exported 249 bales, or 38,695 lbs., or nearly twenty times that quantity. He thought he might fairly say that if we succeeded in repressing the slave-trade, as he believed we should, we should in a few years receive a very large supply of this most important article from the West Coast of Africa.

MR. J. H. GURNEY said:

As to the growth of cotton in Central Africa, he had received from Mr. Thomas Clegg, of Manchester, a few figures, from which it appeared that while in 1852 only 1800 lbs. of cotton had been brought into Great Britain, the quantity increased in 1856 to 11,500 lbs., in 1857 to 35,400 lbs., and in the first five months of the present year it was 94,400 lbs. Mr. Clegg further stated that the quality of this cotton, between December, 1856, and April, 1858, had been such that its average price had reached within one half-penny that of the middling quality of cotton brought from New Orleans. At the same time the native manufacture was carried on to a considerable extent, so that within a particular period 200,000 pieces had been exported to Brazil, 200,000 pieces were sent to the people living beyond the cotton-producing districts, while the inhabitants of those districts had themselves been kept supplied. Another abundant article of produce which had not yet made its way into this market, but which must do so before long, was indigo. It was extensively grown in the countries bordering on the cotton district, and it only required a continuance of the present system to develope the export of that produce.

MR. BUXTON said:

There was no question now, that any required amount of cotton, equal to that of New Orleans in quality, might be obtained. A very short time ago Mr. Clegg, of Manchester, aided by the Rev. H. Venn, and a few other gentlemen, trained and sent out two or three young negroes as agents to Abbeokuta. These young men taught the natives to collect and clean their cotton, and sent it home to England. The result was, that the natives had actually purchased 250 cotton-gins for cleaning their cotton, and lately these natives of Abbeokuta had sent to England and procured four presses for pressing it for exportation, at a cost of several hundred pounds. Mr. Clegg stated that he was in correspondence with seventy-six native and other African traders, twenty-two of them being chiefs. With one of them Mr. Clegg had a transaction, by which he (the African) received 3500*l*. And the amount of cotton received at Manchester had risen, hand over hand, till in 1856 it came to 35,000 lbs., and last year to nearly 100,000 lbs. Well might Mr. Clegg say, that this was "a rare instance of the rapid development of a particular trade, and the more so because every ounce of cotton had been collected, all the labor performed, and the responsibility borne by native Africans alone." The fact was, that the West African natives were not mere savages. In trade no men could show more energy and quickness. And a considerable degree of social organization existed. He could give a thousand proofs of this, but he would only quote a word or two from Lieutenant May's despatch to Lord Clarendon, dated the 24th of November, 1857. Lieutenant May crossed overland from the Niger to Lagos, and he says:

"A very pleasing and hopeful part of my report lies in the fact, that certainly three-quarters of the country was under cultivation. Nor was this the only evidence of the industry and peace of the country; in every hut is cotton spinning; in every town is weaving, dyeing; often iron smelting, pottery works, and other useful employments are to be witnessed; while from town to town, for many miles, the entire road presents a continuous file of men, women, and children carrying these articles of their production for sale. I entertain feelings of much increased respect for the industry and intellect of these people, and admiration for their laws and manners."

LORD PALMERSTON said:
I venture to say that you will find on the West Coast of Africa a most valuable supply of cotton, so essential to the manufactures of this country. It has every advantage for the growth of that article. The cotton districts of Africa are more extensive than those of India. The access to them is more easy than to the Indian cotton districts; and I venture to say that your commerce with the Western Coast of Africa, in the article of cotton, will, in a few years, prove to be far more valuable than that of any other portion of the world, the United States alone excepted.

THE CULTIVATION OF COTTON IN AFRICA.

PAPERS relative to the cultivation of cotton in Africa have been presented to the British House of Lords by command of the Queen. They include two reports on the subject from Mr. Consul Campbell (of Lagos) to the Earl of Clarendon, dated respectively the 5th of January and the 14th of March, 1857. An account is also given of the trade of the Bight of Benin for the year 1856, and it hence appears that the whole of the Yoruba and other countries south of the Niger, with the Houssa and Nuffee countries on the north side of the same river, have been from all time cotton-growing countries; and that, notwithstanding the civil wars, ravages, disorders, and disruptions caused by the slave-trade, more than sufficient

cotton to clothe their population has always been cultivated, and their fabrics have found markets and a ready
sale in those lands where the cotton plant is not cultivated, and into which the fabrics of Manchester and
Glasgow have not yet penetrated. The cultivation of
cotton, therefore, in the countries already named is not
new to the inhabitants; all that is required is to offer
them a market for the sale of as much as they can cultivate, and by preventing the export of slaves from the
seaboard, to render some security to life, freedom, property, and labor. It is estimated that the annual cultivation of cotton in Yoruba and the adjacent states, is
equal to 7,200,000 pounds. Whenever the cotton fabrics
of England are introduced, via the Niger, to the upper
part of the Yoruba and the circumjacent districts, the
natives will probably sell their own cotton and clothe
themselves with the lighter and cheaper cloths of Manchester and Glasgow. There is no hope of inducing the
natives to cultivate coffee, because it is a "new thing,"
(the Africans being obstinately conservative,) and would
require care, attention, intelligence, and, above all, pa-
tience. Cotton alone, therefore, can be looked to as an
agricultural marketable production, obtainable from the
interior of Africa. Meanwhile English cotton fabrics
are gradually working their way into Africa and super-
seding the native manufacture. The two greater staples
of the trade of the Bight of Benin are palm-oil and ivory,
cotton ranking as the third.—*London Times.*

CAPE COAST CASTLE COTTON.

A LETTER received by the Cotton Supply Association
from Mr. R. D. Ross, Cape Coast Castle, Gold Coast,
states emphatically that cotton, which is indigenous to

Africa, and grows abundantly in Ashantee, might be obtained equal to that of Georgia, both in quantity and quality. The natives have from time immemorial woven their own clothes, but now prefer those of Manchester. Mr. Ross thinks the Africans would readily profit by instruction, and that Africa would ere long compete with the slave states of America, if capitalists would establish an organization in central districts to purchase and prepare for export all the cotton which the natives should be left to grow themselves.—*London Anti-Slavery Reporter.*

LETTER FROM THE REV. ALEXANDER CRUMMELL.

EFFORTS are being made by the Liberian Government and citizens to foster and induce the cultivation of cotton. The extent of the present attempt may be perceived from the subjoined extract from a letter to the author, dated Monrovia, April 10th, 1858, from the Rev. Alex. Crummell:

I am much interested by a new movement in our rural districts this farming season ; and, as I am aware of a like interest on your part, I cannot let the next American mail depart without dropping you a few lines concerning it.

During the last rainy season, some few of us spent a portion of our time in speechifying and lecturing upon agriculture. During the recent fair, likewise, the same subject, in general, came prominently before the public. As my share in this matter, I have dwelt much upon roads and cotton planting. I have reason to believe that some of my hopes and desires, in both these respects, are in the way of being fulfilled and gratified.

1. During the last six months there has been one almost universal inquiry for cotton seed. Men have

been despatched to the country for it; the British consul has been applied to, and the few citizens who have had small patches, have been beset by their neighbors for even the smallest contributions. .

2. At the commencement of the year, I took occasion to visit nearly every farmer on the St. Paul's River, to ascertain whether there was likely to be any real result from the inquiry and interest I had observed in our communities. In answer to my questions I obtained, not the pledge, but the declaration from many farmers, from Millsburg to Caldwell, that they intended to plant cotton this season; some spoke of one acre, others of two, and several of more. Such was the interest exhibited, that I called upon the President, to see whether I could not get a 'Convention' on the river, and the pledge of some twenty or thirty men, that they would each plant this season, three or five acres—have gins prepared for the cotton—and a press at hand, so that the cotton might not lie unused upon the soil for months, or perhaps a year or two. *For in this little point lies the whole question of success or non-success of cotton-planting in Liberia.* If the man who plants one or two acres, can sell his picked cotton at once, he will plant more next year. If it lies upon his hand a year unused and unproductive, then it is a point of demonstration to him that cotton-planting is a failure in Liberia.

Some little has been done; one of my friends has planted ten acres, another three, another two, several one; Mr. Warner five. As far as I can get returns, there are about fifty acres of land now planted with cotton in this, Montserrado County, and perhaps twenty more will be added.

P. S. April 19th.—Since I wrote the above, I have heard of eight more acres of cotton: some on the Junk River, in a new farming region, just opened.

COTTON FROM LIBERIA.

In May, 1850, John Pender, of London, with S. Gurney, the London banker, and some gentlemen of this neighborhood, entered into an undertaking for the purpose of endeavoring to ascertain the possibility or otherwise of procuring a supply of cotton from the African coast. Having obtained letters of introduction from Lord Palmerston for Mr. J. K. Straw, to whom the charge of the expedition was intrusted, to the admiral of the station, Mr. Beacroft, and to President Roberts, of Liberia, they purchased two small ships, and freighted them with general merchandise, sending out, at the same time, a quantity of New Orleans cotton seed. Eight small bags of cotton, the fruit of this experiment, have recently arrived in Manchester, consigned to Mr. Fleming, of the Manchester Commercial Association, by Mr. Pender, who is a member of this body. The cotton is white and good, and is valued at 5d. per pound. In every way it is suitable to the wants of the manufacturers. The experiment has shown to a demonstration that good cotton can be grown in Liberia without any difficulty, and it is the intention of the conductors of the enterprise to persevere in it.

London Times.

EFFORTS MADE BY PRESIDENT BENSON.

So very certain am I, that this can be demonstrated to be one of the most advantageous cotton-growing countries in the world, as that I feel impatient that its capacity in that be properly tested, and though we are in the midst of a severe pecuniary pressure, yet I cannot forego the idea of recommending that this government offer and pay a premium of one hundred dollars annually, for the next four years, to the person who will in Liberia produce from one acre of land, in each successive year, the largest quantity of the best quality of cotton ; the sum of sixty dollars for the largest quantity of second quality of cotton, and forty dollars for the largest quantity of third quality of cotton, each quality of the produce of a single acre. The extending of the time to four successive years of annual competition, will be a great inducement for competitors to plant the first year, from the fact that the cotton plant being perennial with us multiplies and extends its branches so rapidly, as that in a well-cultivated field, each plant will increase not much less than a hundred per cent. in its annual yield, at least for the first four years; which fact will evidently give the advantage in the fourth to those who will have been diligent to plant the first year.

The very commendable interest that is being manifested by a respectable number of our citizens of both sexes from the several counties of this Republic, who design being exhibiters and competitors at the national fair to commence in this city on the 14th inst., fully satisfies my mind that such a measure would prove a great stimulus to a number of our citizens to test the cotton-growing capacity of this country, by actual experiment of systematic cultivation; which I doubt not would demonstrate to us facts far surpassing our most sanguine expectations; thus directing the attention of our citizens to a rich and inexhaustible source of wealth as yet untouched, which by a proper manly development would greatly augment the interest between this State and Europe, and would perhaps more than anything else affect for good the future condition of millions of our race, as well as rapidly elevate us as a nation in the estimation of the civilized world.

It affords me pleasure to be able to say that H. B. M.

Consul residing here will, from the very lively interest he feels in this matter, engage to furnish seed of the best quality to as many as may wish to try the experiment with *foreign* cotton seed. He has received from the Manchester Cotton Supply Association, within the past few weeks, a series of pertinent questions relative to the mode of cotton cultivation in Liberia, and the capacity of the country to produce that article on an extensive scale, which questions, for aught we know, may lead to the most happy results in the future, mutually beneficial to both countries.

I deny that a fair trial has ever been made at cotton-growing to any extent in Liberia by the Americo-Liberians. Those who have tried it on a small scale in their yards and gardens well know that it so far exceeded their highest expectations in yield and quality as to have astonished them. In like manner, if a fair trial was given to it on a large scale, properly cultivated in suitable soil which abounds with us, would far transcend any idea we had formed of its profitableness.—*Annual Message, Dec.*, 1857, *of President Benson of Liberia.*

(From the Philadelphia North American of September 27th, 1858.)

COTTON CULTIVATION IN AFRICA.

DURING the last ten years, Western Africa has been making the most rapid progress. Trade has been striking root, and promises in a short time to become of immense value. It has been demonstrated that the forty or fifty millions of inhabitants of that region are an industrious race. Some of them are noted for their mercantile intelligence, enterprise, and success. Instances have been given in which a native merchant laid out fifty thousand dollars in the course of a single year, in the purchase of goods, the money having been remitted before the goods were sent, while another had spent thirty thousand dollars.

It has been calculated that, between 1830 and 1850, the increase of the exports of British manufactures to that part of the coast lying between the Senegal and the Portuguese colony of Loando, amounted to one hundred per cent., and since that time the progress made has been much more rapid. Between 1850 and 1856, the total exports from Great Britain increased forty per cent., and during the same six years the imports of African produce into England have increased sixty per cent. Palm-oil, timber of valuable kinds, ivory, gold, groundnuts, indigo, pepper, rice, coffee, sugar, and a multitude of other articles, are only waiting a market to be produced in any quantities. The trade in palm-oil is already valued at ten millions of dollars per annum. But the most important prospect is that of the supply of cotton. It is already manufactured there to a considerable extent. Brazil is reported to have imported last year a quantity of African made cloths, which it would require upwards of seven million pounds of cotton to produce. In 1856, 33,495 pounds of cotton were sent from Abbeokuta. This amount increased in 1857 to 55,400 pounds; and in the first six months of the present year, it reached upwards of 100,000 pounds. "The whole of this has been collected, all the labor performed, and the responsibility borne by native Africans alone."

The American portion of the population of Liberia have commenced, with much spirit, the cultivation of cotton. About seventy acres of land, in patches of from one to ten acres, are planted in Montserrado County. One of a party of emigrants, belonging to Columbus, Georgia, sent home lately from Liberia a sample of cotton, of a species which heads all the time, and he says, good sea-island cotton can be grown there. Native labor is cheap and abundant.

The subjoined extract, from a recent letter from President Benson, will tend to show what is doing, and that it is the intention of the Liberians to persevere in the cultivation of our great staple:

MONROVIA, July 13th, 1858.

MY DEAR SIR:

*   *   *   *   *   *   *   *   *   *

You have the cordial thanks of Liberians for the interest you have manifested for the development of the agricultural resources of this country, especially cotton cultivation. Anything like premiums from the Manchester Cotton Supply Association would prove a great stimulus to that department of industry. I fully indorse your every sentiment on the policy of Liberia exerting herself to become a cotton-producing country. Nothing will tend more to strengthen the bonds between Great Britain and our republic, and raise it in the scale of respectability. I have been laboring industriously, ever since I have been in office, to secure this object. I have striven to keep the subject constantly before our people. I encourage them by all possible justifiable means; and I am happy to say that I now feel encouraged. The inhabitants of the four counties of this Republic have gone earnestly to work at it. There has been twenty times more cotton planted by Americo-Liberians this year than ever before, of both native and foreign seed, and I feel sanguine that its cultivation will increase each succeeding year.

We received by the May steamer one half ton of cotton from England from the Manchester Cotton Supply Association. Notwithstanding it arrived two months after the proper season, yet I have distributed it to each county long since, and the inhabitants have planted somewhat extensively, but nothing to compare with what they will do next year, when they will have plenty of seed at the proper planting season. I repeat that whatever comes from England in the way of premiums will be highly appreciated, and will, in my opinion, have the desired effect.   *   *   *   *

Most respectfully, your obedient servant,

STEPHEN A. BENSON.

LIBERIAN MARINE.

T͟HE brig George C. Ackerly is expected to sail from New York on the 10th of August, for the West Coast of Africa. The Ackerly is the property of Mr. E. J. Roye, colored, of Monrovia, and is engaged as a trader along the African seaboard. This is another indication of the growth of the commerce of Africa, and of the enterprise of the Liberians. There are some forty small vessels engaged in the coast trade of Liberia, built and owned in that Republic. Besides these, the firm of Mc-Gill Brothers (colored men), own and run two schooners of some hundred tons each. One of these, the "President Benson," has recently sailed from Baltimore, homeward bound, with a valuable cargo.—*Public Ledger.*

OPENING OF AFRICA.

WHILE England is seeking to reach the head waters of the Niger, by steaming up that stream, the people of Liberia are about to send an exploring party overland interiorward, into the valley of that mighty river. This region of the continent is the great native caravan route. Two of these were recently seen, one of which could not have contained less than five thousand persons and one thousand beasts of burden. The Government of Algeria is striving to establish a direct and constant intercourse with Central Africa. The French calculate, that under advantageous circumstances, the trade with that region would be worth sixty millions of francs annually, or ten millions of dollars, the bulk of which would consist of actual barter.

It is computed that there are in Africa five hundred missionaries, one thousand native helpers, fifty thousand church members, and thirty-five thousand children in mission schools. The slave-trade has been almost entirely suppressed along the West Coast for two thousand miles. Those busy hives of industry, Senegal, Gambia, Sierra Leone, the Republic of Liberia, the Gold Coast settlements, Lagos, Abbeokuta, Fernando Po, Bonny, Calabar, the Bights of Benin and Biafra, the Cape of Good Hope, Natal, Mozambique, and the results that must ensue from the Zambesi exploration under Livingstone, will contribute their share to the regeneration of Africa. These powerful agencies are rapidly building upon the soil an independent negro nationality. They are opening up the hitherto unknown land to commerce, through which untold material wealth will be poured into the lap of Christendom, by the exchange of the products of human industry.—*Public Ledger.*

SLAVE POLICY IN AFRICA.

The leading men of the Southern States of America are gradually being convinced that cotton can be successfully and profitably raised in Africa, and are advocating the organization, with white masters, of the institution of slavery in that country. This course is boldly proclaimed in the course of a series of letters lately published by the celebrated General Duff Green. From these the following extracts are taken:

"Who can read the account of the explorations of Central Africa, by Livingstone, and note the imposing manner in which he has been sent back, with an extraordinary outfit and escort, and hesitate to believe that extraordinary efforts will be made to get a supply of cotton *from Africa*, at less cost than it can be obtained from us? How can that be done? *By maintaining the status of African slavery in Africa ; and sending the white master to the black slave, instead of bringing the black slave to the white master.*

Who so ignorant of European policy as not to see that England is apprehensive that France will absorb the African states, and by conquests in Central Africa, build up an African empire, and that the question between France and England is soon to be which is to become the largest owner of African slaves, and the boldest advocate of African slavery? Who cannot see that their purpose is to colonize Africa, and that if South Carolina does re-open the slave-trade, she must purchase French or British subjects, under a French or a British license? Let no one be startled at these anticipations of the future. It is the duty of statesmen to foresee that which is to be, by a careful analysis of the present and the past. In confirmation of this I refer to Mr. Bowen, a native of Georgia, and altogether reliable, who, as a missionary, has penetrated the interior of Africa. He tells me that there are millions of slaves, some of them held by semi-civilized masters; that the climate and soil are suited to the culture of sugar and cotton, and that the price of slaves is from twelve to fifty dollars! I refer, also, to the late proceedings of the Manchester Cotton Supply Association, which show that they look with much hope and confidence to that quarter, and especially to the country in the rear of Sierra Leone and Lagos.

Is it not, therefore, apparent that the real question is *who shall command the market?* Our planters in the South, or French or British planters in Africa—our planters, with lands at twenty dollars per acre and slaves at one thousand dollars per head, or French or British masters in Africa, with lands as a gratuity and slaves at fifty dollars each? The fact is new, but it is no less true because it is new."

CULTIVATION OF COTTON IN AFRICA.

To THE EDITOR OF THE NEW YORK TIMES:
It is no longer a matter of doubt that cotton can be largely cultivated in Central Africa. The Rev. T. J. Bowen, the indefatigable missionary and explorer of that region, has set this question at rest. Not only is cotton of a superior quality grown there, but it is so well adapted to that soil that it springs up spontaneously. It is also a perennial, and requires much less labor than it does in our own country. From the accounts which have recently been published, it appears that it has become an article of export to Great Britain. If this culture should be greatly enlarged there, we see no reason why the slave-trade may not thus be peacefully extinguished. If this result can be thus reached, the civilized world will rejoice. It seems that already the cultivation of cotton and the trade in palm-oil have extirpated the slave-trade from many districts in Central Africa. The exports of palm-oil from the Bight of Benin last year were to the value of $10,000,000. It is, then, by the development of lawful commerce that the traffic in slaves will cease.

This truth is gaining access to the minds of intelligent colored men at the North, and an organization has been already formed to carry out their views. An expedition to explore Yoruba will start this fall, and it is hoped that ere long a civilized community of enterprising colored Americans will be engaged in the cultivation of cotton, sugar, rice, coffee, &c., and the production of palm-oil,

4

in that healthful and fertile country. All will rejoice at such manifestations of enterprise among our colored population. Yoruba is situated west of the Niger and north of the Bight of Benin.

A description given by the Rev. Mr. Bowen, who has been five years a resident and Baptist missionary in Yoruba, is as follows: "Between Abbeokuta and the Niger, that is within a distance of 160 miles, there are more than a dozen large towns, some of which are more populous than Abbeokuta. Central African houses are built in Moorish style, large and low, with many rooms opening into an interior court. The walls are made of clay, which bakes hard in the sun, and the roofs are generally thatched with grass. In some respects, the Soudanese are considerably advanced from mere barbarism. Whether heathens or Mohammedans, they are clad in trowsers and tunics. They are remarkably courteous in their social intercourse. Several rude arts are commonly practised, as the smelting of iron, and in some places of copper and lead; the manufacture of hoes, axes, adzes, knives, and swords; the spinning of cotton and silk; weaving and tailoring, both of which are regular professions; dyeing blue, yellow, and red; soapmaking; brewing corn and millet; making palm and grass hats, also saddles, bridles, and sandals, and a sort of shoes and boots. Three towns in Nufe have the art of working in glass. But the great business of the people is agriculture, in which they are far more skilful and industrious than we have supposed. The principal crops are Indian corn, the same as our own, and the tropical yam. But they also plant cotton, sugar-cane, beans and peas, sweet potatoes, cassava, ground peas, ginger, red pepper, &c., and the country is admirably adapted to coffee and other tropical productions of great value to the civilized world.

"Yoruba is a healthy and fertile region; that it is well adapted to the cotton and sugar culture; that it is the key to Central Africa, and the yet unvisited *gold regions* of Soudan; that it is wide open to missionary influences; and that there is room for hundreds of thousands of enterprising colonists. The mere enunciation of these facts opens out a vast field for contemplation. We wonder that enterprising men of color do not perceive the directing hand of Providence in all this. Here is a field for the development of Anglo-African energy and talent. Why should not the inexhaustible riches of Soudan be brought into use at some future time? The natives would soon supply any demand which a legitimate commerce would create. Untold wealth exists but a few hundred miles in the interior of Africa, which can be developed upon the introduction of a Christian civilization."

HOPE FOR AFRICA.

THE recent discoveries that have been made of the fertile resources of Africa, her vegetable products and gold deposits, and the almost impossibility of the available development of these by the white race, give presage of an extensive colonization of the colored race at no very distant day. This will not probably be so much a benevolent as commercial movement. The subjects of it will be the free colored population of America; the agents of it will be chartered or voluntary companies; the object of it will be more gain upon the part of man; but the end of it, under the controlling hand of God, will be the civilization of Africa. The Philadelphia Bulletin, in an interesting article on this prospective African exodus, says:

"There is every inducement for it. Recent works on Africa show that the country is of inexhaustible vegetable wealth, that common industry is there repaid as it is nowhere else, and the free black, depressed by white European rivalry in this country, may there become a man of standing and authority.

There is one thing, however, which will impel such an exodus towards Africa, as we have long waited for and hoped to see. In Africa, the richest gold deposits in the world await the miner. We have been assured by a gentleman whose integrity we are willing to vouch for, and who has been eighteen years in the Guinea trade, that the amount of gold which abounds in some places, and which is protected by superstitious taboo and by "fetish" notions from being gathered, is literally incredible. All that has been found in California or Australia is as nothing, compared to what will yet be gathered from the obscure regions of Africa. A thousand facts confirm our assertion; anecdotes and hints in a score of books, old and new, as well as geological proof, tend to show that gold is there in *immense* quantities.

We may remark, in conclusion, on the vast amount of good which gold is doing towards settling the world. Regions most inaccessible and remote are becoming peopled, and opening markets to the earlier world. What if gold, that is called the root of all evil, should be the destined agent to civilize Africa, induce an emigration of free blacks from this country, and improve the whole race! *What* is impossible in the nineteenth century?"

In republishing the above article from the "Evening Bulletin," of this city, for the purpose of making known all the available wealth of Africa, the author desires expressly to object to the idea of any necessity for an exodus of our colored population.